EMMA Jane TidESWELL.

eMMA   Jane   Tide Swell

Alpha Press Pte Ltd., Singapore © 1972

First published in Singapore in 1972 by
Alpha Press Pte Ltd., Singapore.
First published in Great Britain in 1977 by
Macdonald and Jane's Publishers Limited
Paulton House
8 Shepherdess Walk
London N1 7LW
ISBN 0 354 08026 1

Printed in Singapore by Toppan Printing Co (S) Pte Ltd

Folktales from the Orient

General Editor: Eileen Colwell

the bird hunter

an indonesian folktale

Retold by Chia Hearn Chek
Illustrated by Kwan Shan Mei

MACDONALD AND JANE'S · LONDON

Raja Ishak, the ruler of the land, loved archery.
While his friends were discussing other subjects,
he never stopped talking about bows and arrows
from sunrise till sunset.
Soon, everyone came to know
of the King's love for archery.

Now the King had a very beautiful daughter
called Bintang Devi.
She was so beautiful that it was the wish
of every young man to marry her.
But Raja Ishak let it be known that
only the best archer in the country
should marry his daughter.

So one day the King decided to hold an archery contest
to decide the matter.
Many men from far and near came
to take part in the contest.
But no one won the prize, for even among so many
the king could not find a great archer.

Now in this land there lived a poor bird hunter
by the name of Wajan.
He heard that Raja Ishak had a beautiful daughter
who would marry only the most skilful archer in the country.
Wajan thought that it would be wonderful
if he could marry the Princess, so he made a clever plan.
He caught some wild birds with a net.
He then killed the birds and took out the right eye of each.
Wajan tied the birds up with string
and hung them from a pole.
Then he made his way to the Palace.
On the way, he shouted,
"One-eyed birds for sale! One-eyed birds for sale!"
Soon children began to follow him
for they had never seen a man selling one-eyed birds before.

As he went,
Wajan shouted continually,
''One-eyed birds for sale!
One-eyed birds for sale!''
At last, he arrived
at the gate of the Palace.
The King, seeing a crowd
of children at his gate,
sent a servant to see
what was the matter.

The servant returned and said,
''Your Majesty, it is only a poor bird hunter
selling one-eyed birds.''
On hearing this, the King said,
''Send the man in at once.''
So Wajan was brought before the King.
''Is it true that the birds you are selling
all have only one eye?'' Raja Ishak asked.
''Yes, Your Majesty, I always shoot my birds in the eye
with my bow and arrow,'' replied the poor hunter.

Raja Ishak was very surprised.
He could hardly believe his ears.
"Young man, it is not an easy matter
shooting birds in the eye with an arrow.
You must be the greatest archer in the country,"
the King said.
"A great archer like you should have a beautiful wife.
Would you like to marry my daughter?"
The bird catcher replied at once,
"But, Your Majesty, I am only a poor bird hunter.
Where can I get the money to give your daughter
the kind of life she is used to?"

"Ah, not only are you a great archer,
I see you are also an honest man.
As a king, I can give you all the money you need.
And as for a house, why, you can move into the Palace,"
said the King.
Wajan was very happy when he heard this but
he was careful not to show it.

Not long after, the wedding took place.
Wajan put on the new clothes he was given.
He felt very pleased with himself.
At last, his wish had come true.
Now he had everything —
a beautiful Princess for a wife
and a home in the Palace.

At the wedding, there was a big feast.
Raja Ishak invited many of his friends to come.
It was a beautiful day.
Birds of every colour were flying in the sky.
The food was good and the musicians had never played better.
Everyone was enjoying himself.
Suddenly, overcome with excitement, the King jumped up and said,
''Listen! Now the great archer will show us
his skill with the bow and arrow.''

On hearing this, Wajan nearly fainted.
When he had recovered from the shock, he said,
‘‘Your Majesty, much as I would like to show you my skill,
I’m afraid I can’t as I left my bow and arrow
at home when I came here.’’
Wajan thought that he had given a clever answer.

But the King was not to be put off. He said,
"That does not matter at all, you may use mine,"
and he sent a servant to fetch his bow and arrow.
All this time Wajan was shaking with terror
for he knew he would soon be found out.
Just then the servant returned with the King's bow and arrow
and Raja Ishak thrust them into the hunter's hands.
"There you are," said the King, "show us your skill."

Now Wajan had never used a bow and arrow before.
Slowly he drew the string and pointed the arrow to the sky,
then he stood there afraid to release it.
Birds were flying all over the sky and the people began to wonder
why the great archer did not shoot down even one.
Some began to laugh at him openly.
One said, "Look, he's afraid.
He can't even hold the bow and arrow properly!"

At last, one man lost his patience. He walked up
to the hunter and slapped him hard on the back, saying,
''Shoot now, great archer!''
The hard slap on his back made Wajan release the arrow
just as a crane was flying by. The arrow hit the bird
and it fell to the ground dead.

Raja Ishak picked up the bird and was amazed to see that
the arrow had pierced the crane's narrow neck.
"You are indeed the greatest archer I have ever seen," he exclaimed.
Everyone was astonished. But Wajan pretended to be very angry.
"I'll never touch a bow and arrow again."
He said loudly, "As I have said before,
I always shoot my birds in the eye and not in the neck.
If someone had not hit me on the back,
I would certainly have shot the crane in the eye."
The King at once punished the man
who had hit the hunter on the back.

As for Wajan, he never had to touch
a bow and arrow again, so everyone believed
he was the greatest archer in the country.

The Editor

After gaining her Diploma of Librarianship at University College, London, Eileen Colwell spent two years at Bolton Library before moving to Hendon in North London in 1926. There was no library service for children there at that time, so she started one; three years later she was Borough Children's Librarian, and today Hendon Children's Library is famous in many parts of the world – a tribute to a pioneer in the field of children's reading. When the new Borough of Barnet was formed, Miss Colwell continued as Librarian in charge of work with children, with an even larger number of schools and libraries under her care.

Eileen Colwell is past-Chairman of the International Federation of Library Associations' committee on Library work with children, and she has been a member of the Carnegie Medal Committee of the Library Association since its first award in 1936.

Storytelling has always been her special interest and joy, and it has taken her to many parts of Britain, Holland, the United States and Canada. Her unique services to children's libraries and books, both at home and abroad, received recognition in the 1965 New Year Honours, when she was awarded the M.B.E. Now in retirement, Miss Colwell devotes all her time telling stories and lecturing on children's literature up and down the country.

The Author

Chia Hearn Chek is probably Southeast Asia's best known writer of children's books. Trained as a teacher, he was awarded a U.S. Department of State grant to the University of Michigan English Language Institute to do a specialised course in English Language teaching in 1960. Five years later he was awarded a British Commonwealth Bursary to the University of London Institute of Education to study publishing and book production. In 1969 he was again sent on a UNESCO award to the Tokyo Book Development Centre to specialise in children's literature. He has represented his country on many occasions at international conferences and seminars on children's book writing and was a consultant to the UNESCO Mobile Training Team on Book Development in Asia for the years 1975 and 1976. His works in the Moongate Collection published in several languages are the first of their kind to appear in this part of the world and have proved to be highly successful both at home and in the international market. Besides telling children's stories, Hearn Chek's other passion is art and his one other love is music.

The Illustrator

Born in Peking, Kwan Shan Mei studied art at an early age under the great Chinese master Chow Han Mei in Shanghai after which she worked as a magazine illustrator till she moved to Hongkong where her talents were much in demand both by the press and the book publishers. She came to Singapore to take up the post of Art Director in a multinational publishing house in 1965. Kwan Shan Mei has done extensive research work in Oriental costumes and her illustrations have won her both international and local awards — receiving Honourable Mention in the Bratislava International Children's Book Competition (BIB '73), a gold as well as a silver medal for the Best Designed Book of the Year competition in the 1974 Singapore Festival of Books and more recently another gold medal in the 1975 Festival. A highly versatile artist, she now freelances although much of her time is occupied with the Moongate Collection of which she is the major illustrator.